Rumpelstiltskin

First published in 2008 by
Franklin Watts
338 Euston Road
London
NW1 3BH

Franklin Watts Australia
Level 17/207 Kent Street
Sydney
NSW 2000

Text © Anne Walter 2008
Illustration © Peter Cottrill 2008

A CIP catalogue record for this book is available
from the British Library.

ISBN 978 0 7496 7902 6 (hbk)
ISBN 978 0 7496 7908 8 (pbk)

Series Editor: Melanie Palmer
Series Advisor: Dr Barrie Wade
Series Designer: Peter Scoulding

Printed in China

Franklin Watts is a division of
Hachette Children's Books,
an Hachette Livre UK company.

HOPSCOTCH
FAIRY TALES

Rumpelstiltskin

by Anne Walter and Peter Cottrill

W
FRANKLIN WATTS
LONDON•SYDNEY

Once upon a time, a poor, foolish
miller lived with his daughter.

The miller wanted to please the king. So, one day, he took his daughter to the king's palace.

"My girl can spin straw into gold," the miller lied, boastfully. The king was pleased. He loved gold.

The king took the girl to a room full of straw. "Spin this into gold by morning, or you will die!" he ordered, locking the door.

The girl started to cry. She had no idea how to spin straw into gold, or how to spin anything!

Then a funny little man appeared.
"What's the matter?" he asked.
"I must spin all this straw into
gold," the girl told him.

"If I help you, what will you give
me?" asked the little man, smiling.
"Take my necklace," she replied.

The little man took the necklace
and sat at the spinning wheel
until all the straw had been turned
into gold. Then he vanished.

When the king saw the gold, he
was amazed. But he wanted more.

The king took the girl to a bigger
room with even more straw.
"Now spin all this straw into gold,"
he ordered, locking the door again.
Once more, the girl started to cry.

Then the funny little man returned.
"If I help you, what will you give
me this time?" he asked.
"Take my ring," she replied.

Again, the man spun the straw
until the room gleamed with gold.
Then he vanished.

When the king saw the gold, he was delighted, but he wanted more.

The king took the girl to a huge room, bursting with straw. "Spin this straw into gold, and I will make you my queen," he promised.

As the girl wept, the little man returned. "I will help you, but what will you give me?" he asked. The girl had nothing left.

"After you become queen, you will give me your first child," he told her. Then he spun all the straw into gold.

The king kept his promise and made the girl his queen. Later, she had a beautiful baby boy.

Then the little man came back for his reward. "I will have your child, just as you promised," he said. "Oh please don't take my child," sobbed the queen.

The man felt sorry for the queen. "Let's play a game," he said. "If you can guess my name, you can keep your child. You have three days."

On the first day, the queen guessed:

"Is it Roger or Peter?

Barry or Harry?"

"No! None of them," laughed
the little man. "Two days left!"
he said and skipped away.

On the second day, the queen tried stranger names. "Is it Rumbleweed, Twistybeard, or Cleverchops?"

"No, No, No!" he laughed again.
"One day left," he said and
vanished.

The queen needed help, so she sent out some spies. Deep in the forest, they heard a little man singing.

"Ha, ha, the queen will never win,

She'll never guess I'm ...

Rumpelstiltskin!"

On the third day, the queen said:
"Hello ... Rumpelstiltskin!"
The little man was so shocked
he could not speak.

He stamped his feet and bit his hat,

then disappeared and that was that!

Hopscotch has been specially designed to fit the requirements of the Literacy Framework. It offers real books by top authors and illustrators for children developing their reading skills. There are 55 Hopscotch stories to choose from:

* hardback